Feet, Go to Sleep

by **Barbara Bottner**

illustrated by **Maggie Smith**

Alfred A. Knopf
New York

For the children who don't have their own bed to sleep in,
the beautiful children of Schools on Wheels
—B.B.

For Sam & Ida, and with love and thanks
to Harridy Ansky for taking me to the beach!
—M.S.

THIS IS A BORZOI BOOK PUBLISHED BY ALFRED A. KNOPF

Text copyright © 2015 by Barbara Bottner
Jacket art and interior illustrations copyright © 2015 by Maggie Smith
All rights reserved. Published in the United States by Alfred A. Knopf,
an imprint of Random House Children's Books, a division of Random House LLC,
a Penguin Random House Company, New York.
Knopf, Borzoi Books, and the colophon are registered trademarks of Random House LLC.
Visit us on the Web! randomhouse.com/kids
Educators and librarians, for a variety of teaching tools, visit us at RHTeachersLibrarians.com

Library of Congress Cataloging-in-Publication Data
Bottner, Barbara.
Feet go to sleep / by Barbara Bottner ; Illustrated by Maggie Smith. — First edition.
    p.   cm.
Summary: A child looks back on the day and drifts
off to sleep, one body part at a time.
ISBN 978-0-449-81325-6 (trade) —
ISBN 978-0-449-81326-3 (lib. bdg.) — ISBN 978-0-449-81327-0 (ebook)
[1. Bedtime—Fiction. 2. Sleep—Fiction.] I. Smith, Maggie, illustrator. II. Title.
PZ7.B6586Fe 2014   [E]—dc23   2012045972
The illustrations in this book were created using watercolor, gouache, fabric, and digital media.
MANUFACTURED IN CHINA   May 2015   10 9 8 7 6 5 4 3 2 1   First Edition
Random House Children's Books supports the First Amendment
and celebrates the right to read.

"Time to say good night," said Mama.
"I'm not ready!" said Fiona.
"You've had a long day.
You must be tired, from your head
to your toes," said Mama.
"Maybe just a *little* tired. . . ."

"Toes, go to sleep!" said Fiona.

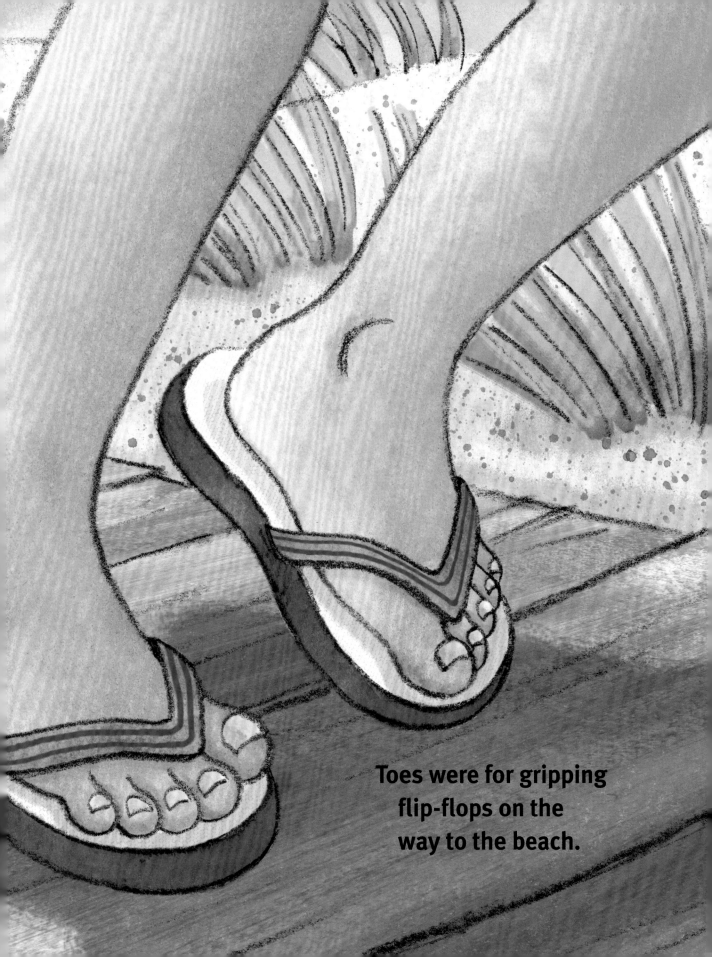

Toes were for gripping
flip-flops on the
way to the beach.

Toes were easy. They went right to sleep.

"What's next?" asked Mama.

"Feet, go to sleep!"

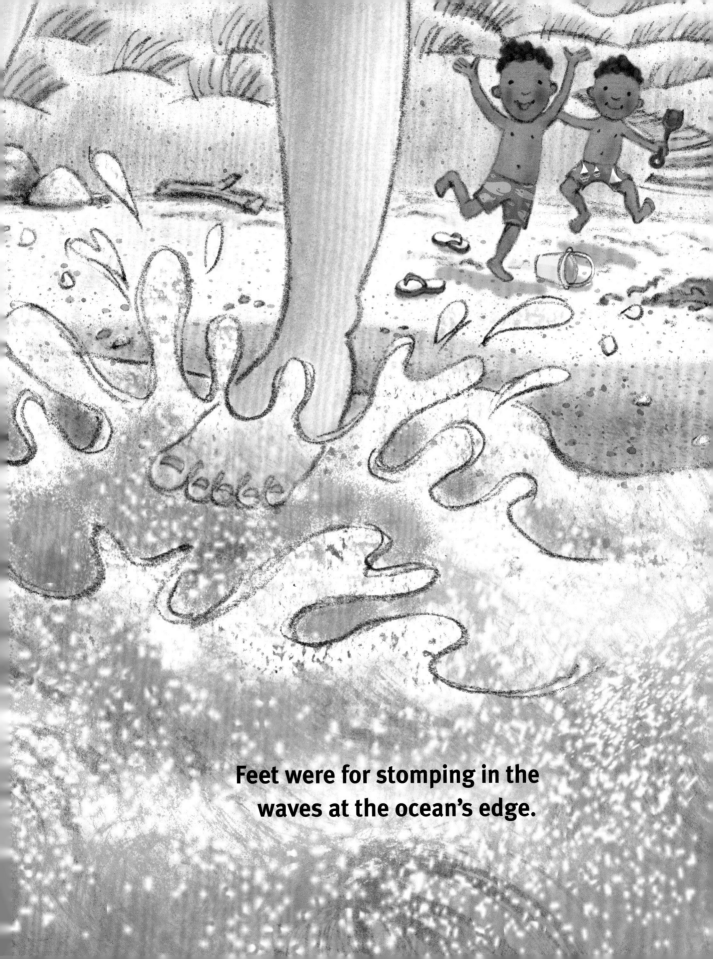

Feet were for stomping in the waves at the ocean's edge.

Feet *were* tired.

"You're getting good at this," said Mama.

"Knees, go to sleep!"

Knees were for staying steady while building a sand castle.

"Legs, go to sleep."

Legs were for running
after the cousins.

Now Fiona's legs became heavy, and then very still. "Legs have had a long day," said Mama. "Keep going."

"Tummy, go to sleep," said Fiona.

Tummy was for all the yummy strawberries!

"Shoulders, go to sleep," said Fiona, giving them one last roll before they lay still.

Shoulders were for rubbing with sunscreen.

"Arms, go to sleep."

Arms were for catching the beach ball. And throwing it, too.

And what about hands? And fingers?

"Arms, hands, fingers, do as
you are told, please."
Fiona's arms were weary and
drifted into a toasty sleep.

What's left?
Fiona wondered.

"Mouth, go to sleep,"
said Fiona with
a little yawn.

Mouth was for remembering the tang of mustard on hot dogs.

"Ears, go to sleep!"

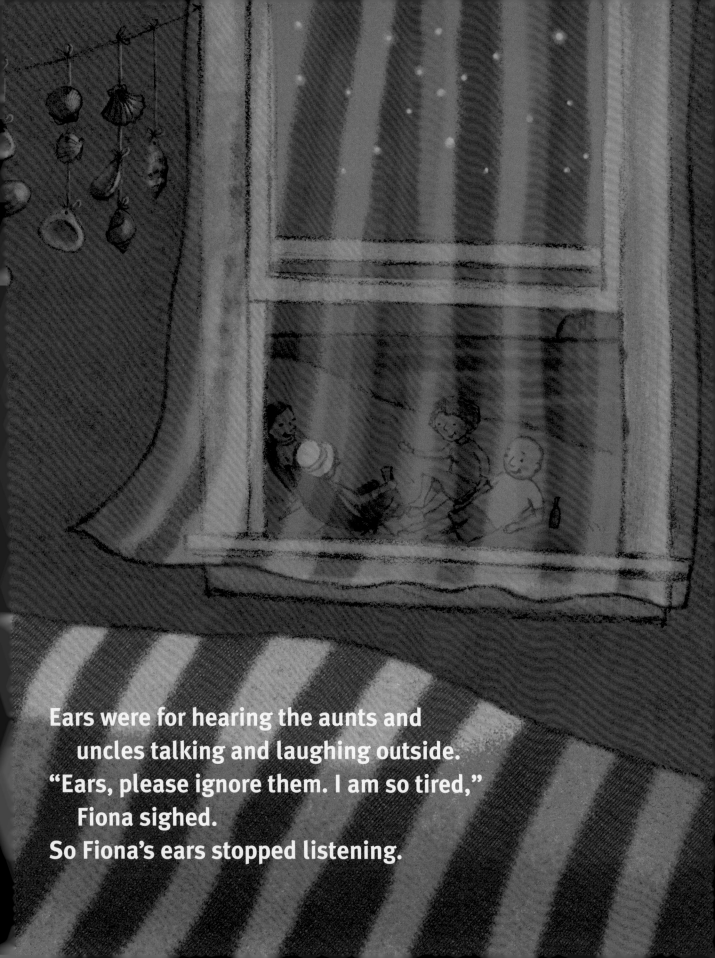

Ears were for hearing the aunts and
    uncles talking and laughing outside.
"Ears, please ignore them. I am so tired,"
    Fiona sighed.
So Fiona's ears stopped listening.

"Eyes, go to sleep," whispered Fiona.
    She shut them tight.
    But Fiona's monkey mind was still awake.
So many memories of the wonderful day . . .
    "Go to sleep . . . ," Fiona mumbled to herself.
    "Go to sleep . . . Fiona, go to sleep."